DATE DUE

DORR H	9 - 5 - '78		
KLA. R C	4 - 1 0 '80		
KLA. R B	9 - 8 - '80		
FORKS A	9 9 81		
WIL C A 2	2 '82		
FT. JO D 2	2 4 '83		

This edition first published 1975 by Lerner Publications Company
Illustrations copyright © 1975 by George Overlie
International Standard Book Number: 0-8225-0283-6
Library of Congress Catalog Card Number: 72-12489
Manufactured in the United States of America

LIFE ON THE MISSISSIPPI

THE BOYS' AMBITION

by Mark Twain

pictures by GEORGE OVERLIE

Lerner Publications Company • Minneapolis, Minnesota

WHEN I was a boy, there was but one permanent ambition among my comrades in our village[1] on the west bank of the Mississippi River. That was, to be a steamboatman. We had transient ambitions of other sorts, but they were only transient. When a circus came and went, it left us all burning to become clowns; the first negro minstrel show that ever came to our section left us all suffering to try that kind of life; now and then we had a hope that, if we lived and were good, God would permit us to be pirates. These ambitions faded out, each in its turn; but the ambition to be a steamboatman always remained.

[1]Hannibal, Missouri

Once a day a cheap, gaudy packet arrived upward from St. Louis, and another downward from Keokuk. Before these events, the day was glorious with expectancy; after them, the day was a dead and empty thing. Not only the boys, but the whole village, felt this. After all these years I can picture that old time to myself now, just as it was then: the white town drowsing in the sunshine of a summer's morning; the streets empty, or pretty nearly so; one or two clerks sitting in front of the Water Street stores, with their splint-bottomed chairs tilted back against the walls, chins on breasts, hats slouched over their faces, asleep—with shingle-shavings enough around to show what broke them down; a sow and a litter of pigs loafing along the sidewalk, doing a good business in watermelon rinds and seeds; two or three lonely little freight piles scattered about the "levee"; a pile of "skids" on the slope of the stone-paved wharf, and the fragrant town drunkard asleep in the shadow of them; two or three wood flats at the head of the wharf, but nobody to listen to the peaceful lapping of the wavelets against them; the great Mississippi, the majestic, the magnificent Mississippi, rolling its mile-wide tide along, shining in the sun; the dense forest away on the other side; the "point" above the town, and the "point" below, bounding the river-glimpse and turning it into a sort of sea, and withal a very still and brilliant

the clerks wake up, a furious clatter of drays follows, every house and store pours out a human contribution, and all in a twinkling the dead town is alive and moving. Drays, carts, men, boys, all go hurrying from many quarters to a common center, the wharf. Assembled there, the people fasten their eyes upon the coming boat as upon a wonder they are seeing for the first time. And the boat *is* rather a handsome sight, too.

SHE is long and sharp and trim and pretty; she has two tall, fancy-topped chimneys, with a gilded device of some kind swung between them; a fanciful pilot-house, all glass and "gingerbread," perched on top of the "texas" deck behind them; the paddle-boxes are gorgeous with a picture or with gilded rays above the boat's name; the boiler-deck, the hurricane-deck, and the texas deck are fenced and ornamented with clean white railings; there is a flag gallantly flying from the jack-staff; the furnace doors are open and the fires glaring bravely; the upper decks are black with passengers; the captain stands by the big bell, calm, imposing, the envy of all; great volumes of the blackest smoke are rolling and tumbling out of the chimneys — a husbanded grandeur created

with a bit of pitch-pine just before arriving at a town; the crew are grouped on the forecastle; the broad stage is run far out over the port bow, and an envied deck-hand stands picturesquely on the end of it with a coil of rope in his hand; the pent steam is screaming through the gauge-cocks; the captain lifts his hand, a bell rings, the wheels stop; then they turn back, churning the water to foam, and the steamer is at rest.

Then such a scramble as there is to get aboard, and to get ashore, and to take in freight and to discharge freight, all at one and the same time; and such a yelling and cursing as the mates facilitate it all with! Ten minutes later the steamer is under way again, with no flag on the jack-staff and no black smoke issuing from the chimneys. After ten more minutes the town is dead again, and the town drunkard asleep by the skids once more.

MY father was a justice of the peace, and I supposed he possessed the power of life and death over all men, and could hang anybody that offended him. This was distinction enough for me as a general thing; but the desire to be a steamboatman kept intruding, nevertheless. I first wanted to be a cabin-boy, so that I could come out with a white apron on and shake a tablecloth over the side, where all my old comrades could see me; later I thought I would rather be the deck-hand who stood on the end of the stage-plank with the coil of rope in his hand, because he was particularly conspicuous. But these were only day-dreams—they were too heavenly to be contemplated as real possibilities. By and by one of our boys went away. He was not heard of for a long time.

At last he turned up as apprentice engineer or "striker" on a steamboat. This thing shook the bottom out of all my Sunday-school teachings. That boy had been notoriously worldly, and I just the reverse; yet he was exalted to this eminence, and I left in obscurity and misery. There was nothing generous about this fellow in his greatness. He would always manage to have a rusty bolt to scrub while his boat tarried at our town, and he would sit on the inside guard and scrub it, where we all could see him and envy him and loathe him.

And whenever his boat was laid up he would come home and swell around the town in his blackest and greasiest clothes, so that nobody could help remembering that he was a steamboatman; and he used all sorts of steamboat technicalities in his talk, as if he were so used to them that he forgot common people could not understand them. He would speak of the "labboard" side of a horse in an easy, natural way that would make one wish he was dead. And he was always talking about "St. Looy" like an old citizen; he would refer casually to occasions when he was "coming down Fourth Street," or when he was "passing by the Planter's House," or when there was a fire and he took a turn on the brakes of "the old Big Missouri"; and then he would go on and lie about how many towns the size of ours were burned down there that day.

Two or three of the boys had long been persons of consideration among us because they had been to St. Louis once and had a vague general knowledge of its wonders, but the day of their glory was over now. They lapsed into humble silence, and learned to disappear when the ruthless "cub"-engineer approached. This fellow had money, too, and hair-oil. Also an ignorant silver watch and a showy brass watch-chain. He wore a leather belt and used no suspenders. If ever a youth was cordially admired and hated by his comrades, this one was. No girl could withstand his charms. He "cut out" every boy in the village.

When his boat blew up at last, it diffused a tranquil contentment among us such as we had not known for months. But when he came home the next week, alive, renowned, and appeared in church all battered up and bandaged, a shining hero, stared at and wondered over by everybody, it seemed to us that the partiality of Providence for an undeserving reptile had reached a point where it was open to criticism.

This creature's career could produce but one result, and it speedily followed. Boy after boy managed to get on the river. The minister's son became an engineer. The doctor's and the post-master's sons became "mud clerks"; the wholesale liquor dealer's son became a barkeeper on a boat; four sons of the chief merchant, and two sons of the county judge, became pilots. Pilot was the grandest position of all. The pilot, even in those days of trivial wages, had a princely salary—from a hundred and fifty to two hundred and fifty dollars a month, and no board to pay. Two months of his wages would pay a preacher's salary for a year. Now some of us were left disconsolate. We could not get on the river—at least our parents would not let us.

SO, by and by, I ran away. I said I would never come home again till I was a pilot and could come in glory. But somehow I could not manage it. I went meekly aboard a few of the boats that lay packed together like sardines at the long St. Louis wharf, and humbly inquired for the pilots, but got only a cold shoulder and short words from mates and clerks. I had to make the best of this sort of treatment for the time being, but I had comforting day-dreams of the future when I should be a great and honored pilot, with plenty of money, and could kill some of these mates and clerks and pay for them.

MARK TWAIN

American humorist Mark Twain was born Samuel L. Clemens on November 10, 1835, in Florida, Missouri. Although Twain was destined to become one of America's most celebrated writers, his boyhood dream was to become a river-boat pilot on the Mississippi. This dream was in fact fulfilled in 1859. Two years later, however, with the outbreak of the Civil War, Twain quit his job as a steamboat pilot and began his long career as a writer. Using "Mark Twain" as his pen name, he wrote such classics as *A Connecticut Yankee in King Arthur's Court*, *The Prince and the Pauper*, and *The Adventures of Huckleberry Finn*—his masterpiece. "The Boys' Ambition" comes from *Life on the Mississippi*, an autobiographical work written in 1883. In it, Twain recalls his dream of becoming a steamboatman on the Mississippi, the river that remained forever linked with him.